One day, when Peter w[...]
heard a knock at the wi[...]
"Who could that be?" he wondered.

"Could we put our tent in your yard?" asked Duck. "Sure," said Peter. "But please be careful. There's a family already living here."

Everyone helped to put up the tent —
except...

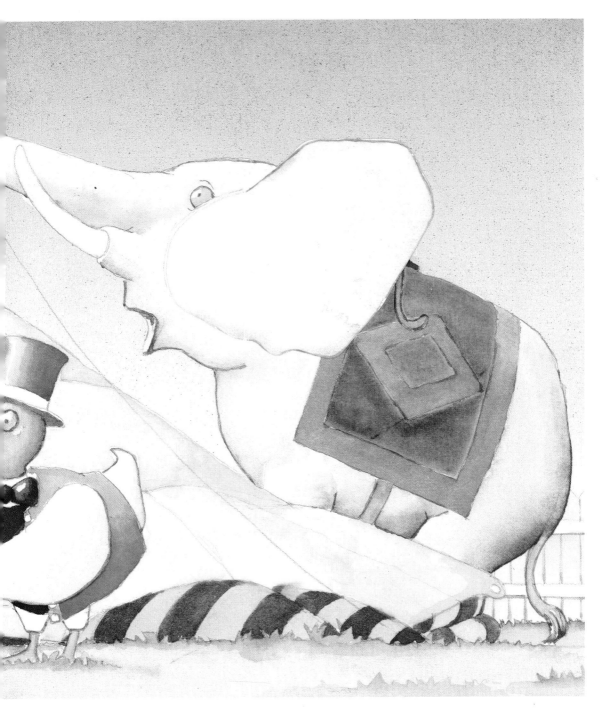

"Which act will I be in?" asked Peter.
"Look in the sea lion's suitcase," answered Duck.

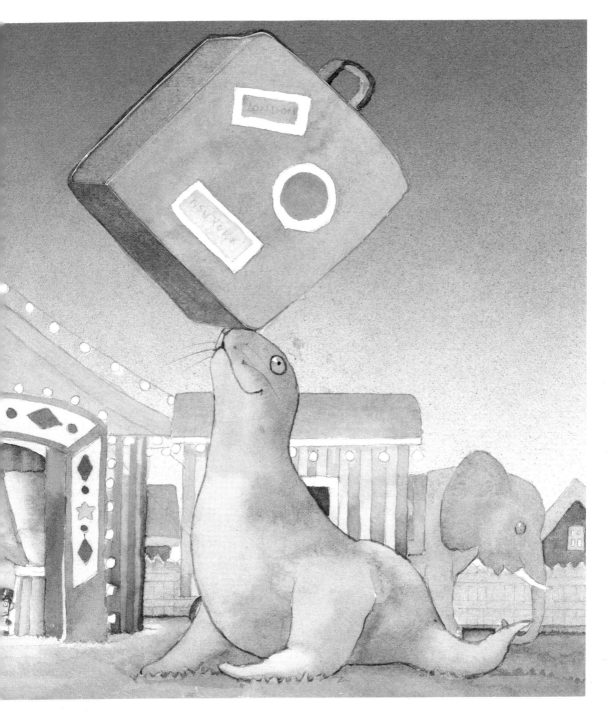

All of Peter's friends came to the circus.
What would the first act be?

Duck pulled doves out of his hat —
without cheating, of course!

Next came the tallest monkey in the world!

Finally — the big clown act!

But where was Monkey?

After the show, everyone went home to bed.
Except Monkey. He was still wide awake!